THE HALF&HALF DOG

HALF DOG

written and illustrated by
LISA GROSS

LANDMARK EDITIONS, INC.
P.O. Box 4469 • 1402 Kansas Avenue • Kansas City, Missouri 64127
(816) 241-4919

Dedicated to

all people who have ever wanted to be
loved and accepted as they are;
and to everyone who has
encouraged me to write,
especially my mother Andrea.

Fourth Printing

COPYRIGHT© 1988 BY LISA GROSS

International Standard Book Number: 0-933849-13-3 (LIB.BDG.)

Library of Congress Cataloging-in-Publication Data
Gross, Lisa, 1974-
   The half & half dog.
   Summary: Scorned and ridiculed for his unusual appearance, a dog, half of which
looks like a golden retriever and half a Scottie, begins a search for acceptance and a
sense of self-worth.
   [1. Dogs — Fiction.]
I. Title.   II. Title: Half and half dog.
PZ7.G8995Hal   1988   [Fic]   88-9347

Editorial Coordinator: Nancy R. Thatch
Creative Coordinator: David Melton
Production Assistant: Dav Pilkey

Landmark Editions, Inc.
P.O. Box 4469
1402 Kansas Avenue
Kansas City, Missouri 64127
(816) 241-4919

Printed in the United States of America

THE HALF & HALF DOG

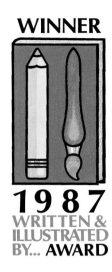

When Lisa learned her book had not won in the 1986 NATIONAL WRITTEN & ILLUSTRATED BY... AWARDS CONTEST FOR STUDENTS, she immediately sat down and started writing another book for the 1987 CONTEST. Her determination certainly paid off, because our national panel of judges chose that book as WINNER of the 10 to 13 age category.

I wasn't surprised when Lisa's book won, because during preliminary review of entries, the judges' reactions were always so enthusiastic. "There's something very special about this book," one judge told me. When I finally read THE HALF & HALF DOG, I wholeheartedly agreed.

There is indeed a special quality about Lisa's book. Throughout the narrative there flows an underlying thoughtfulness and sensitivity for those who look different from others. The half-and-half dog's search for acceptance and the discovery of his own sense of self-worth have both universal appeal and a personal message. And I think readers will be impressed with Lisa's ability to explore the serious elements in her story, even within episodes of broad humor.

I was fascinated by Lisa's development of the drawings for her book. Although the illustrations in the book she submitted in the CONTEST were nicely drawn and colored, when she began preparing final illustrations for publication, I was delighted to witness a metamorphosis of skills and imagination in her work.

In my job as Creative Coordinator, I try to discover the natural approaches of our illustrators, then show them professional techniques that will improve their skills. Lisa was able to immediately incorporate such techniques in her drawings. Soon she challenged me to teach her more. Within weeks I forgot Lisa's age and began working with her in the same way I would work with an adult professional — which she seemed to appreciate and enjoy.

The result is a book, thoughtfully developed and skillfully presented with an excellent blend of text and illustrations. And I shall no longer keep you from enjoying Lisa's delightful book.

—David Melton
Creative Coordinator
Landmark Editions, Inc.

When Davey Robinson stepped into the garage that morning, he let out a shriek.

"They're here!" he yelled excitedly. "Louisa's had her puppies!"

Davey's mother and father ran to the doorway. His four-year-old sister Sarah wasn't far behind.

"How many puppies are there?" Sarah wanted to know.

"One, two, three, four, five, six!" Davey exclaimed.

"Three are golden retrievers — just like Louisa," Mrs. Robinson noticed.

"And the other three are black," Mr. Robinson remarked. "Just like the Scottie that lives down the street."

"Aren't they cute!" Sarah giggled.

"They're beautiful!" Mrs. Robinson agreed. "Good girl," she said, stroking Louisa's silky head. "You've done a fine job."

Louisa proudly wagged her tail, while she gently cuddled her puppies against her side.

As the Robinsons watched the newborns, they suddenly heard a muffled whimper come from behind Louisa. Davey peeked over Louisa's back to see what had made the noise.

"You're not going to believe this," he announced. "There's one more puppy."

"Is it brown, or is it black?" Sarah asked.

"It's both," Davey replied with a puzzled look on his face.

"Does it look like Louisa or the Scottie?" Mrs. Robinson inquired.

"Well," Davey said, scratching his head in disbelief, "it looks like Louisa *and* it looks like the Scottie too — depending on which way you look at it."

"What on earth are you talking about?" his mother said impatiently.

"Well, folks, prepare yourselves for a surprise, because you've never seen anything like this," Davey replied. Then he reached down, picked up the seventh puppy, and held it up for everyone to see.

"Oh, no!" Mrs. Robinson gasped.

"What kind of a dog is that?" Sarah wanted to know.

"It's the weirdest kind of dog I've ever seen," Davey said.

And they all agreed, it *was* strange — because one half of the puppy looked like a thoroughbred golden retriever, but the other half was a pure black Scottie.

"He looks like someone drew a line down his middle and divided him into two parts," Mr. Robinson said, shaking his head.

"I think he looks like someone sewed two dogs together," Sarah said, squinting her eyes and making a face.

"Well, no one will want to buy this one," Mr. Robinson said in disgust. "We'll probably have to take him to the dog pound."

"But he's so unusual!" Davey exclaimed. "Can't we keep him?"

"No way!" his mother and father answered together, and then they turned and walked back into the house.

"He sure is ugly," Sarah remarked as she took another look.

"You can say that again," Davey agreed.

"Sure is ugly," Sarah repeated.

After Davey and Sarah had left the garage, Louisa looked down at her little puppy.

"The brown side isn't so bad," she thought. "And the black side isn't too bad either." However, even Louisa had to agree that the two sides together did look different — yes, even strange.

"But no matter what, he *is* my baby," Louisa said. Then she sighed a motherly sigh and gently licked her puppy's forehead — on the golden retriever side, of course.

During the weeks that followed, Louisa tried to give the half-and-half puppy the same love and attention she offered to her other puppies. But his brothers and sisters were not so kind. The brown puppies didn't like the black side of the half-and-half pup. And the black puppies didn't like his brown side.

"You are so ugly!" the other puppies would tell him.

Whenever Louisa heard her puppies say such an unkind thing, she scolded them. But as soon as her back was turned, they would scowl at the half-and-half puppy and whisper, "Ugly! Ugly! Ugly!"

When the puppies ate, the black ones lined up on one side of the bowl and the brown ones ate from the other side. But no matter which side the half-and-half pup tried to use, the others edged him away from the bowl. Most of the time he had to wait until his brothers and sisters had eaten their fill. Then he was allowed to eat whatever was left.

When the puppies were eight weeks old, Mr. Robinson placed a "PUPPIES FOR SALE" sign in the front yard. For several days buyers came into the garage to look at the puppies. Some liked the brown puppies best. Others were more interested in the black ones.

The half-and-half puppy tried to attract attention by rolling over and wiggling his tail. But Mr. Robinson's prediction was right — people were eager to buy his brothers and sisters, but no one wanted the puppy that was a golden retriever on one side and a black Scottie on the other.

As soon as the other puppies were sold, Mr. Robinson wasted no time. Without even giving the half-and-half dog a chance to say good-bye to his mother or letting Louisa give her puppy a final lick of affection on his golden retriever ear, the man picked up the puppy and put him in a box. Then he put the box in the back seat of the family car.

"He sure is ugly," the half-and-half dog heard Sarah say, as the car rolled out of the driveway.

The little puppy already missed his mother. He shivered, and one big, lonely tear swelled up and ran down his black Scottie cheek.

If the man at the dog pound thought the half-and-half dog looked strange, he didn't say so. He just took the puppy from the box and carried him inside. At the end of a dark hallway, the man opened an iron gate and placed the puppy on the floor of a large cage.

"Shut up!" the man yelled, when the other dogs in the pound started to bark. Then he slammed the iron gate shut and snapped the lock in place.

When the half-and-half puppy looked around, he saw iron bars on all sides of the cage and wire mesh covering the top of the cell.

"Hey, punk!" a surly voice called from the shadows at the back of the cage.

The half-and-half dog froze with terror.

Out of the shadows stepped two ferocious-looking dogs. They were big, mangy, ragamuffin mutts with mean sneers on their faces. One scraggly mutt had a big black patch over one eye. The other dog had a bandaged leg and limped as he walked.

"What kind of a dog is that?" Black Patch growled.

"Beats me," Lamebone replied as he limped forward.

The mutts came closer and closer. The puppy shivered with fright and backed into a corner of the cage.

"Sure is ugly!" Black Patch snarled.

"So ugly it hurts my eyes to look at him," Lamebone said.

"Mine too," Black Patch agreed.

"What do you think we should do with this punk?" Lamebone asked, smiling an evil grin.

The half-and-half puppy's heart beat faster and faster. His mouth felt dry and his nervous little legs shook so hard he could barely stand up.

Suddenly the biggest, most vicious-looking dog the puppy had ever seen shoved Black Patch and Lamebone aside. With pointed teeth jutting out of his bottom jaw and his broad shoulders hunched up, a huge bulldog lumbered toward the little pup.

At the sight of this monster, the half-and-half dog almost fainted. He looked around, but there was no place to hide. Then, to his surprise, the bulldog suddenly turned and faced the two mutts.

"You guys back off!" the bulldog ordered. "If you want to pick on someone, then pick on someone your own size. Can't you see this little fella's only a pup? He's scared to death. Leave him alone!"

"Aw, Max, we wasn't really gonna hurt him," said Black Patch. "We was just teasin' him a little."

"Scram!" commanded Max.

Grumbling to each other, and with their tails tucked between their legs, Black Patch and Lamebone slunk to the back of the cage.

Max looked down at the puppy. "If they try to give you a bad time, little fella," he said, "you just tell Max about it. I'll take care of them."

"Yes, Sir," the puppy said gratefully, and he gave a deep sigh of relief.

From that time on, Black Patch and Lamebone never again threatened the puppy. But just the same, the puppy didn't stray far from Max's side. The half-and-half dog scampered at Max's heels all day long. He even tried to copy his hero's heavy-footed shuffle. And at night, the puppy would rest his head against the bulldog's shoulder.

One night the half-and-half dog was awakened by the sound of voices. When he opened his eyes, he realized Max and the two mutts were in the far corner of the cage, whispering about something. He couldn't hear everything that was being said, but he did hear Max say ". . . before the guard can get up, we'll be out the door and on our way."

The half-and-half puppy jumped up and walked over to Max. "What's going on?" he wanted to know.

"We're planning our escape," Max said under his breath.

The little puppy's ears perked up. "Escape!" he exclaimed.

"Shhhhhhhh!" Max ordered. "We don't want anyone to hear us."

"When do we go?" the excited puppy whispered.

"Not you, kid," Max said firmly. "Just me and the other two guys are breakin' out."

"But, can't I go too?" the puppy asked.

"You're too little," the bulldog replied. "When we get out that door, we'll run like greased lightning . You wouldn't be able to keep up with us."

"But, I can run real fast," the puppy insisted.

"Not fast enough, kid," Max told him.

The puppy was silent for a moment. Then he asked, "May I at least help you?"

"Come to think of it, we could use your help," Max answered.

"Anything," the puppy agreed.

"Okay, here's what we need you to do," Max whispered, moving closer to the puppy. "In the morning, when the guard brings our food, as soon as he opens the gate, we want you to start yapping and running around. While he's busy watching you, the mutts and me will knock him down and hightail it out of this joint. Do you think you can do that, little fella?"

"Yes, I can," said the determined puppy.

"Okay," Max concluded, "our escape is planned. We'd better get some sleep."

Black Patch and Lamebone settled down where they were. Max and the half-and-half dog returned to their corner of the cage.

"I really want to go too," the puppy said, hoping Max might change his mind.

"No, kid," Max replied, "you'd better stay here where you'll get fed regularly. Life on the streets would be too tough for a little guy like you. Besides, it won't be long before a real nice family comes and takes you home with them."

"I don't know if that will ever happen," the puppy sighed.

"Sure it will," Max told him.

"You're the best friend in the whole world," the puppy said to Max.

"You're okay, too, kid," the bulldog replied quietly.

Black Patch and Lamebone were already asleep, and soon Max was snoring. But the half-and-half dog couldn't sleep. He was too excited. Over and over he thought about his part in the escape. He wanted to be sure he would remember exactly what to do.

Early the next morning, when the guard came down the hallway carrying a large bowl of food, Max and the two mutts pretended they were still asleep. As

planned, the half-and-half dog was stationed close to the gate, ready to spring into action.

The closer the guard came, the faster the half-and-half dog's heart beat. The puppy heard the guard slip the key into the lock and turn the handle.

Then something terrible happened! When the guard stepped inside, the half-and-half dog's mind went completely blank, and he forgot what he was supposed to do.

But Max didn't hesitate. The big bulldog lunged forward and grabbed the guard's leg in his powerful jaws. Following Max's lead, Black Patch and Lamebone leaped up, hit the guard in the chest, and knocked him to the floor.

The bowl filled with food flipped out of the guard's hands and flew high into the air. Food scattered everywhere, and when the bowl came down, it landed upside down on top of the half-and-half dog. The puppy huddled underneath for protection and stayed out of sight. Max and the mutts wasted no time. They bolted out the gate and raced down the hall.

The half-and-half dog peeked out from beneath the bowl in time to see the guard run down the hall and out of the building. Then he noticed the guard had forgotten to shut the cage gate.

Still crouched under the bowl, the puppy crept slowly and quietly out of the cage and down the hall. When he reached the door, he stopped and cautiously looked out from his hiding place. The guard was nowhere in sight . . . and . . . the front door was standing WIDE OPEN!

"Should I, or shouldn't I?" the puppy wondered.

"I will!" he decided, and without another moment's hesitation, the half-and-half dog crawled from beneath the bowl, darted through the doorway and sped across the parking lot.

The puppy ran down the sidewalk as fast as his legs could carry him. When he came to the street corner, he didn't stop to look left or right, but raced straight across the street. A screech of brakes frightened him, and if he had known how close a car had come to hitting him, he would have been frightened even more. With his heart pounding harder and harder, the puppy ran swiftly, weaving around people's legs and dodging their feet.

When the half-and-half dog came to the next street, he suddenly stopped. Directly in front of him was the truck from the dog pound. The guard was seated behind the steering wheel, looking for Max and the others.

The puppy thought quickly. He scurried under a parked car and stayed there. As the truck moved forward, the puppy saw that the guard had already found two of the escapees. Caged in the back of the truck, with their heads hung low, stood Black Patch and Lamebone. The puppy was glad he didn't see Max in the truck too. His friend was still free!

As soon as the truck turned the corner, the half-and-half dog scooted out from under the parked car and ran in the opposite direction. He turned into an alley and crawled between two trash cans. He hid behind them and tried to catch his breath.

The puppy stayed there for some time, afraid to move or make a noise. He listened for the sound of the guard's truck, but it didn't come his way. Then as his breathing became normal again, the puppy grew drowsy. So he lay down and fell asleep.

The half-and-half dog had no idea how long he had been asleep when he was suddenly awakened by a crash of thunder. A downpour of rain soon followed. He pressed his black Scottie side against the brick building to keep from getting wet, but his golden retriever side was soon soaked to the skin.

Then lightning flashed, and a loud crash of thunder frightened him. He knocked over one of the trash cans as he darted between them. There he stood, shivering and cold. He didn't know which way he should run — he just started running.

The puppy raced down one street and then another, with rain beating against his face so hard he could barely see. But when another bolt of lightning flashed across the sky, he saw a house with a big front porch. He headed straight toward the porch.

When the puppy reached the steps, he scurried under the porch and shook the water from his back. As rain hit against the house, he rested his head between his front paws and thought about his friend, Max. He wondered if Max was still roaming free or if the guard had captured him too.

"This is better than being caged at the pound," the puppy thought, and he moved as far back under the porch as possible. But every time another bolt of lightning flashed and thunder rolled, he wasn't so sure.

Then the half-and-half dog thought about his mother's gentle touch and the warmth of snuggling against her side. And with that thought, the puppy finally fell asleep. There beneath the porch, he spent his first night alone.

The next morning, the half-and-half dog was rudely awakened by the growling of his stomach. After he had yawned, stretched, and scratched an itch that was bothering him, he crawled from under the porch to look for food.

The rain that had washed everything clean had ended. Now bright rays of sunshine warmed the streets and made the grass glisten.

This morning the sidewalks were more crowded with people than they had been the day before. Shoppers were everywhere, and the half-and-half dog had to be extra careful not to get stepped on.

"Fresh vegetables!" the puppy heard a street vendor call. "Step right up and git yer fresh vegetables! Carrots, broccoli, corn on the cob. Cabbage, celery, and farm-fresh lettuce. Step right up an' git yer vegetables!"

The puppy's hunger pangs were growing worse. He ran to the vendor's cart and looked up at the vegetables on display.

"May I help you, Ma'am?" the vendor asked a woman who had stopped in front of the cart.

"I want three pounds of potatoes," the woman replied.

As the vendor weighed the potatoes, the half-and-half dog watched closely. The potatoes didn't look very appetizing to him. In fact, none of the vegetables looked like anything he had ever eaten. He sniffed the air and decided they didn't smell so good either. But the puppy was so hungry, he was willing to try to eat anything.

When the vendor picked up the sack of potatoes from the cart, he accidentally knocked off a long orange thing. The thing had green grassy fringe hanging from one end. The puppy watched it fall.

"What luck!" thought the half-and-half dog. And before anyone could stop him, he grabbed the carrot between his teeth and ran away with it.

As soon as the puppy turned the corner, he stopped and took a big bite out of the carrot. The first bite didn't taste too bad until he started to chew it. Yuck! It was awful! He quickly spit it out.

Now the puppy began to understand what Max had meant when he said, "Life on the streets is really tough."

The puppy's stomach continued to rumble. He had to find something to eat!

In desperation, the half-and-half dog sniffed the air again. He smelled all kinds of odors — fumes from cars, smoke from a cigar, a woman's perfume . . . and then . . . something else.

Mmmmmmm! It was a delicious scent. He sniffed again and began to follow his nose. As the aroma became stronger, the puppy ran faster and faster — straight to the front of a meat market. He peered through the window and saw a store filled with hams, roasts, sausages, and BARBECUED CHICKENS!

"Meat!" the puppy exclaimed. "My favorite food!"

When a customer opened the door and entered the market, the puppy darted inside. The smells inside were even better than they had been outside.

Without hesitating, the half-and-half dog scurried to a table where dozens of barbecued chickens were stacked. He looked up and saw a chicken leg sticking out over the edge of the table. It was the most delicious-smelling thing he had ever smelled in his life. And it was almost within his reach!

While no one was looking, the half-and-half dog stood up on his hind legs, sank his teeth into the chicken leg, and tried to pull it from the table. To his annoyance, he couldn't budge the leg. So the puppy arched his back and tugged even harder. Still he could not pull the leg free.

By now the half-and-half dog was far too hungry to give up. Mustering all of his strength, he yanked with all his might! To his surprise, he got more than a chicken leg. He pulled a whole chicken off the table, which started an avalanche of falling chickens! Dozens of chickens plummeted to the floor and bounced all around the startled puppy.

"Get that dog!" the angry butcher yelled. "Don't let him out!" he tried to warn a customer who was opening the front door.

But the warning came too late. The half-and-half dog dashed between the customer's legs and darted outside. With the chicken gripped in his teeth, he raced down the sidewalk. He didn't stop running until he had reached the safety of his hiding place under the porch.

There the half-and-half dog finally enjoyed his breakfast. It seemed more like a feast to him. And surely it was, because after he had eaten the whole chicken, he wasn't hungry again for the rest of the day.

In the days that followed, the puppy quickly learned which trash barrels in the neighborhood offered special treats — such as crusts of pizza and a variety of bones. And he soon knew what time the butcher threw out scraps.

The puppy enjoyed going downtown. Of course, he learned to look both ways before crossing a street. And he learned how to keep from being stepped on when maneuvering in a crowd of people on a sidewalk.

The half-and-half dog also discovered an interesting thing. When he walked next to a building, and people could see only his black side, they often said, "Oh, look at the cute Scottie!" When he walked in the other direction with only his brown side showing, people would say, "What a pretty golden retriever!"

The half-and-half dog enjoyed hearing kind comments for a change. And he thought it was great fun when people thought they had seen two different dogs. But the puppy soon grew tired of playing such a game.

Then one day, when the half-and-half dog stopped to look through a bakery window at some tasty cakes, he saw an unusual sight. Staring back at him from the other side of the glass was — ANOTHER DOG! And what a strange-looking dog it was! This dog had one shaggy black ear held high in the air and one silky brown ear that flopped down.

The half-and-half dog barked at this strange dog, and to his surprise, the dog barked back at the very same time. Finally the puppy realized that the dog in the window was his own reflection. When he turned his head to the left, he could see his black Scottie side. And when he turned to the right, he saw his golden retriever side.

"Not so bad," the half-and-half dog decided as he looked at each one of his sides.

But then the puppy looked straight forward at his reflection in the window and saw both sides together. For the first time, he realized how strange he looked altogether.

"No wonder everyone laughs at me. I really am a silly looking dog," he said sadly.

The puppy turned away from the window and trudged down the sidewalk. He wished he could find some way to turn his black side into brown or his brown side into black.

"Then," he said, "no one would laugh at me or call me ugly."

The half-and-half dog came to the window of a shoe repair shop and stopped to watch a man who was shining shoes. He saw the man open a tin can and swish a cloth around in some black stuff inside of the can. After the man applied the black goop to a scuffed pair of shoes and rubbed them with a cloth, the shoes became shiny black and looked like new.

"Neat!" thought the half-and-half dog. "The man just rubs the black stuff on and..." The puppy stopped in the middle of his thought and continued to stare at the reflection of his golden retriever side in the window. Then he was struck with a very interesting idea!

When the man turned his back, the puppy darted inside. He quickly grabbed a can of black shoe polish in his mouth and hurried outside.

The puppy carried the can to an alleyway and set it down. Not knowing how to open the can, he started chewing it on the edge. Finally his teeth hit the right spot, and the lid suddenly popped off. What joy!

The half-and-half dog dipped his Scottie paw in the black goop and began to spread it on his golden retriever paw. It worked! Soon that paw was as black as his other one. He rubbed his left hind leg in the polish and started dabbing globs of black stuff all over his brown side and tummy. Next he covered the golden retriever side of his face and smeared black around his floppy brown ear. But he had trouble reaching his back.

The half-and-half dog looked around and saw a post. Aha! He quickly scooped out a dab of black polish and spread it on the post. Then he turned around, pressed his back against the post, and rubbed. Not only did the rubbing back and forth spread the polish all over his back — it satisfied an itch that he couldn't reach.

"Now for the finishing touch!" the puppy said. He wiggled and wagged his tail in the black goop until it, too, was as black as the rest of him.

When the half-and-half dog had finished, he could hardly wait to see the results. Filled with excitement, he raced back to the bakery.

Rearing up on his hind legs, the puppy looked at himself in the window. He turned his head to the right — it was BLACK! He turned his head to the left — now that side was BLACK TOO! He shook his head back and forth — both ears were BLACK! He jumped high into the air — his legs were BLACK! Tail — BLACK! Back — BLACK!

"No more half-and-half dog!" he shouted joyfully. "Now I'm one whole, complete puppy all over!"

"What a cute puppy," the half-and-half dog heard someone say. And without thinking, he turned to see what puppy the man was talking about. He couldn't believe his eyes — the man was pointing at him!

The puppy was so proud that he wagged his all-black tail. Then he turned on his all-black legs and pranced down the sidewalk for everyone to see.

When the puppy turned the corner, a woman in a white dress saw him.

"Oh, look!" the woman exclaimed. "What an adorable puppy!" And she ran to the half-and-half dog, picked him up and wrapped her arms around him.

The puppy loved being adored. He wiggled and squirmed back and forth in the woman's arms, and he wagged his tail with happiness.

Then without warning, the woman screamed and dropped the puppy.

"My dress!" she yelled. "Look at my dress!"

And that's exactly what people did. They stopped and looked at the woman's dress. But now the dress wasn't all white — it was spotted and smeared with black shoe polish.

"It's ruined!" the woman screamed. "That mangy mutt has ruined my dress!" And she ranted and raved on and on. But when she started to kick at him, the puppy scooted across the street and raced for safety under the front porch.

That night the half-and-half dog settled himself down to do some serious thinking.

"If I stay completely black," he reasoned, "no one will say I'm ugly. But no matter what others see, I know that beneath all of this black goop, I have a brown side. And that brown side is a part of me. Still," he thought, "I don't want people to laugh at me and call me names."

Just when the puppy was about to decide to stay black forever, he suddenly thought about Max. Max had seen both sides of him, yet he hadn't laughed or called him names. Max was his friend.

"If Max could like me when I'm half and half," the puppy concluded, "then somewhere in this big world, there must be others who would like the real me."

The puppy didn't know if he could find such friends, but he knew he had to try. If he was a half-and-half dog, then he would live his life as a half-and-half dog. He would be proud of his black Scottie side and just as proud of his golden retriever side.

"No more," the puppy vowed, "will I hide one side of me or the other."

The half-and-half dog went to sleep with only one problem on his mind — "How can I get all this black stuff off of my brown hair?" he wondered.

The next morning, after the puppy had eaten breakfast out of the trash can behind the meat market, he started looking for a way to remove the black shoe polish. While he was crossing a parking lot, something attracted his attention.

The half-and-half dog saw a line of cars being driven into a building. When they entered the building, the cars were very dirty. But when they came out on the other side, they were sparkling clean.

"That should solve my problem!" the puppy exclaimed. So he sneaked over to the line of cars. And when the passengers of a dirty station wagon weren't looking, he scrambled up the back of the car and sat down on top of the luggage rack.

The station wagon was driven to the entrance and the motor was turned off. The puppy watched as a set of tracks in front of the car began to pull the vehicle forward. When the station wagon passed through a curtain of black rubber strips, the puppy eagerly wagged his tail and ducked down.

"This is fun!" thought the half-and-half dog.

Then the tracks stopped moving and everything was silent — but for only a moment. All of a sudden, the track moved the car forward, and bursts of water sprayed at the puppy from every direction. Soapy water stung his eyes, and two huge swirling brushes rolled into action and started knocking him around.

The roar of machines was awful! It hurt the puppy's ears. He grabbed hold of the luggage rack and held on as tightly as he could. At last the station wagon passed the sprays of water, and the brushes stopped.

The puppy hoped his terrible ordeal was over, but it wasn't. Now blasts of clear water shot from all sides, nearly knocking him from the rack. When the sprays stopped pouring, the puppy breathed a sigh of relief.

But there was more to come. Soon noisy blowers began releasing blasts of warm air. The half-and-half dog again held tightly to the luggage rack, as strong currents of air dried the station wagon and his bedraggled body.

Finally the station wagon pulled out of the building, and the exhausted puppy jumped to the ground. As he crossed the parking lot, the half-and-half dog vowed never, ever to go near the car wash again. However, when he looked down at his paws, he was pleased to find that his idea for getting rid of the black shoe polish had worked. Now his left paw was brown again.

And sure enough, as the puppy walked along the sidewalk, people again started to laugh at him. Only now, they laughed even harder than before. Some bent over double with laughter. One man laughed so hard, he had to sit down on the curb and hold his sides.

"Just a bunch of silly people," the puppy told himself, and he tried his best to ignore them. But when he passed a store window and saw his reflection in the glass, he understood why everyone was laughing so hard.

The wind from the dryer had fluffed his hair so high and so full that the half-and-half dog now looked like a FUZZY BALLOON!

The puppy knew that he had to do something to get rid of his fluffy, puffy appearance. So he ran to the park and rolled over and over in the grass until his fur was matted down and back to normal.

"There!" the puppy said. "Not all black . . . not all puffy . . . not anything but myself — the half-and-half dog."

After such a terrifying experience, the puppy enjoyed relaxing in the park. While lying on the grass and feeling the warmth of the sun on his fur, he thought about Max. He wondered where his friend was and what he was doing.

But the puppy's thoughts of Max were soon interrupted by the annoying voices of two boys. He got up and ran over to a stone wall to see what the fuss was about. When he peeked his head around the corner, he saw two tough-looking boys who were teasing a little girl.

"Hey, Carrot Top!" one of the boys said as he pulled the girl's pigtail.

"Don't do that!" the girl cried, trying to pull away.

"What's your name?" the other boy teased. "Is it *Red?* I'll bet you're called *Red.*"

"My name's Lucy. Now please leave me alone!" the girl pleaded, her eyes filling with tears.

But the boy gave Lucy's hair another yank and mocked her. "Oh, look, Red's gonna cry."

The puppy knew he had to help the girl. But how? He remembered how Max had protected him from the mutts in the dog pound. But these bullies were bigger than the mutts, and the puppy knew he wasn't as tough or as strong as Max. He wondered what a little half-and-half puppy could do. Then suddenly, he thought of a great plan!

The puppy jumped upon a park bench and leaped to the top of the stone wall. Ready to begin the first stage of his plan, he turned his black Scottie side toward Lucy and the bullies. Then he pulled back his shoulders and stuck out his chest — just like he had seen Max do. And then he snarled and growled as fiercely as he could.

Lucy and the boys were startled by the sounds. They looked up and saw a black dog that was standing on the wall, growling ferociously and baring his teeth at them.

"What does that dog think he's doing?" one of the boys muttered.

"Let's catch him," the other boy laughed, "and tie a tin can to his tail!"

"Leave that puppy alone!" Lucy cried.

But the boys ran to the wall and tried to grab the dog.

Keeping his black Scottie side turned toward the boys, the half-and-half dog jumped out of the way and scurried along the length of the wall. Then he leaped down and raced across the street, with the bullies following closely behind.

"Catch him! Catch him!" the boys yelled.

When the puppy heard the boys' footsteps drawing nearer and nearer, his heart pounded faster and faster. He swerved around the corner of a building and suddenly stopped. Now, ready to put the second stage of his plan into action, he took a deep breath and turned around. Then he walked nonchalantly toward the boys, making sure they could see only his golden retriever side.

The puppy's plan worked! Since the bullies were chasing a little black dog, they paid no attention to the golden retriever.

"Where did that Scottie go?" the boys yelled as they ran past the puppy and down the sidewalk.

The half-and-half dog couldn't help but feel proud of himself as he headed

back to the park to find the girl. And when the girl saw the puppy coming toward her, she smiled brightly. Then she bent down and patted his head.

"Oh, thank you!" Lucy said. "You really outsmarted those bullies! No regular-looking dog could fool anyone the way you did."

The half-and-half dog felt very happy. He affectionately licked Lucy's cheek.

"You come home with me," Lucy said, taking the puppy in her arms. "I can't wait for my mother to see you. Maybe I can even keep you!"

"A home!" the half-and-half dog thought with excitement. "A real home, just like Max had said."

But then a terrible thought struck him. "What if Lucy's mother doesn't like the way I look? What if she laughs or calls me names?" The puppy grew very quiet.

When Lucy arrived home with the half-and-half dog, she eagerly carried him up the porch steps and opened the door.

"Mommy, come quickly!" Lucy called as she stepped into the living room. "Look what I have!"

When the girl's mother entered the room, she stopped and looked at the puppy. The half-and-half dog closed his eyes and held his breath.

"What an unusual-looking dog!" the mother exclaimed, and she rushed over and patted the half-and-half dog's head. "Where did you find him?"

Lucy told her mother about the two bullies and how the puppy had come to her rescue. And when she told her mother the clever way the half-and-half dog had tricked the boys, they both laughed and hugged the puppy.

"What a smart dog," her mother remarked.

"And he's brave too," Lucy added.

"Well, he certainly looks different from other dogs," her mother said.

"That's what I like about him," Lucy replied. "It makes him special!"

"I think you're right," her mother agreed.

The half-and-half dog could hardly believe his ears.

Smart! Brave! Special!

And better still — Lucy and her mother *liked* him just the way he was — one side a black Scottie and the other side a golden retriever.

"Can we keep him?" Lucy pleaded, her eyes sparkling with anticipation.

"Well," her mother replied, "we'll have to run an ad in the newspaper to see if the puppy belongs to anyone. If no one claims him, he's yours."

"Oh, thank you, Mommy!" Lucy said, and she hugged the puppy again.

The ad was placed in the "FOUND" column of the newspaper. But when no one came to claim the half-and-half dog, Lucy knew he was hers for keeps.

"What are you going to name your puppy?" her mother asked.

"Wow! A name of my own!" thought the half-and-half dog. And he snuggled closer to Lucy and listened intently.

"I've thought about that a lot," Lucy replied. "I don't think names such as Fluffy or Muffin suit him. Those are ordinary names that are fine for ordinary dogs. But my dog is so special, I think he deserves a very special name," she said as she stroked the puppy's fur with her hand.

"Do you have a name in mind?" her mother wanted to know.

The half-and-half dog perked up his ears and listened eagerly.

"Well," Lucy said, "remember when we went to the art museum and saw that unusual painting? You know — the one where half of the woman's face was painted one color and the other half was a different color."

"I remember," her mother replied.

"When I asked you why the artist painted in such an unusual way, you said, 'Because he had the courage to be different.' I think my half-and-half dog has that same kind of courage. So I'm going to name him *Picasso*."

"Perfect!" her mother agreed with a smile.

"And how do *you* like your name, Picasso?" Lucy asked the puppy.

Picasso barked his approval and jumped into Lucy's waiting arms.

una Chandrasekhar
age 9

Anika Thomas
age 13

Cara Reichel
age 15

Jonathan Kahn
age 9

Adam Moore
age 9

slie Ann MacKeen
age 9

Elizabeth Haidle
age 13

Amy Hagstrom
age 9

Isaac Whitlatch
age 11

Dav Pilkey
age 19

by Aruna Chandrasekhar, age 9
Houston, Texas

A touching and timely story! When the lives of many otters are threatened by a huge oil spill, a group of concerned people come to their rescue. Wonderful illustrations.
Printed Full Color
ISBN 0-933849-33-8

by Anika D. Thomas, age 13
Pittsburgh, Pennsylvania

A compelling autobiography! A young girl's heartrending account of growing up in a tough, inner-city neighborhood. The illustrations match the mood of this gripping story.
Printed Two Colors
ISBN 0-933849-34-6

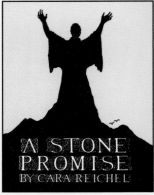

by Cara Reichel, age 15
Rome, Georgia

Elegant and eloquent! A young stonecutter vows to create a great statue for his impoverished village. But his fame almost stops him from fulfilling that promise.
Printed Two Colors
ISBN 0-933849-35-4

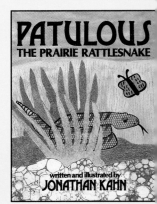

by Jonathan Kahn, age 9
Richmond Heights, Ohio

A fascinating nature story! Whil Patulous, a prairie rattlesnake searches for food, he must try avoid the claws and fangs of his ow enemies.
Printed Full Color
ISBN 0-933849-36-2

by Adam Moore, age 9
Broken Arrow, Oklahoma

A remarkable true story! When Adam was eight years old, he fell and ran an arrow into his head. With rare insight and humor, he tells of his ordeal and his amazing recovery.
Printed Two Colors
ISBN 0-933849-24-9

by Michael Aushenker, age 19
Ithaca, New York

Chomp! Chomp! When Arthur forgets to feed his goat, the animal eats everything in sight. A very funny story — good to the last bite. The illustrations are terrific.
Printed Full Color
ISBN 0-933849-28-1

by Leslie Ann MacKeen, age 9
Winston-Salem, North Carolina

Loaded with fun and puns! When Jeremiah T. Fitz's car stops running, several animals offer suggestions for fixing it. The results are hilarious. The illustrations are charming.
Printed Full Color
ISBN 0-933849-19-2

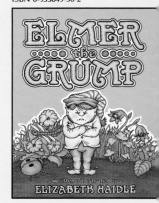

by Elizabeth Haidle, age 13
Beaverton, Oregon

A very touching story! The grumpiest Elfkin learns to cherish th friendship of others after he help an injured snail and befriends a orphaned boy. Absolutely beautifu
Printed Full Color
ISBN 0-933849-20-6

by Amy Hagstrom, age 9
Portola, California

An exciting western! When a boy and an old Indian try to save a herd of wild ponies, they discover a lost canyon and see the mystical vision of the Great White Stallion.
Printed Full Color
ISBN 0-933849-15-X

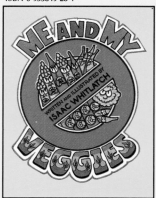

by Isaac Whitlatch, age 11
Casper, Wyoming

The true confessions of a devout vegetable hater! Isaac tells ways to avoid and dispose of the "slimy green things." His colorful illustrations provide a salad of laughter and mirth.
Printed Full Color
ISBN 0-933849-16-8

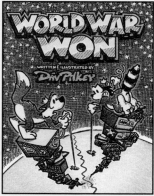

by Dav Pilkey, age 19
Cleveland, Ohio

A thought-provoking parable! Two kings halt an arms race and learn to live in peace. This outstanding book launched Dav's career. He now has seven more books published.
Printed Full Color
ISBN 0-933849-22-2

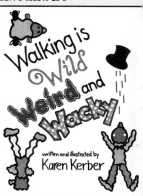

by Karen Kerber, age 12
St. Louis, Missouri

A delightfully playful book! The te is loaded with clever alliterations an gentle humor. Karen's brightly co ored illustrations are composed wiggly and waggly strokes of geniu
Printed Full Color
ISBN 0-933849-29-X

To obtain Contest Rules, send a self-addressed, business-size envelope, stamped with .58 postage, to:

BY STUDENTS!

ILLUSTRATED BY... AWARDS FOR STUDENTS –

by Jayna Miller, age 19
Zanesville, Ohio

The funniest Halloween ever! When Hammer the Rabbit takes all the treats, his friends get even. Their hilarious scheme includes a haunted house and mounds of chocolate.
Printed Full Color
ISBN 0-933849-37-0

by Lauren Peters, age 7
Kansas City, Missouri

The Christmas that almost wasn't! When Santa Claus takes a vacation, Mrs. Claus and the elves go on strike. Toys aren't made. Cookies aren't baked. Super illustrations.
Printed Full Color
ISBN 0-933849-25-7

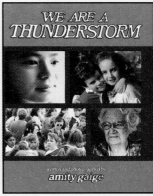

by Michael Cain, age 11
Annapolis, Maryland

A glorious tale of adventure! To become a knight, a young man must face a beast in the forest, a spell-binding witch, and a giant bird that guards a magic oval crystal.
Printed Full Color
ISBN 0-933849-26-5

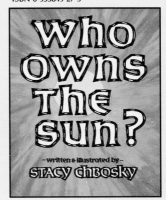

by Amity Gaige, age 16
Reading, Pennsylvania

A lyrical blend of poetry and photographs! Amity's sensitive poems offer thought-provoking ideas and amusing insights. This lovely book is one to be savored and enjoyed.
Printed Full Color
ISBN 0-933849-27-3

by Heidi Salter, age 19
Berkeley, California

Spooky and wonderful! To save her vivid imagination, a young girl must confront the Great Grey Grimly himself. The narrative is filled with suspense. Vibrant illustrations.
Printed Full Color
ISBN 0-933849-21-4

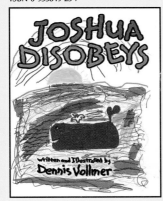

by Dennis Vollmer, age 6
Grove, Oklahoma

A baby whale's curiosity gets him into a lot of trouble. GUINNESS BOOK OF RECORDS lists Dennis as the youngest author/illustrator of a published book.
Printed Full Color
ISBN 0-933849-12-5

by Lisa Gross, age 12
Santa Fe, New Mexico

A touching story of self-esteem! A puppy is laughed at because of his unusual appearance. His search for acceptance is told with sensitivity and humor. Wonderful illustrations.
Printed Full Color
ISBN 0-933849-13-3

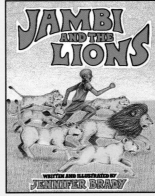

by Stacy Chbosky, age 14
Pittsburgh, Pennsylvania

A powerful plea for freedom! This emotion-packed story of a young slave touches an essential part of the human spirit. Made into a film by Disney Educational Productions.
Printed Full Color
ISBN 0-933849-14-1

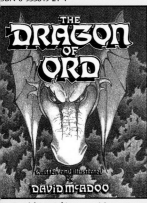

by David McAdoo, age 14
Springfield, Missouri

An exciting intergalactic adventure! In the distant future, a courageous warrior defends a kingdom from a dragon from outer space. Astounding sepia illustrations.
Printed Duotone
ISBN 0-933849-23-0

by Bonnie-Alise Leggat, age 8
Culpeper, Virginia

Amy J. Kendrick wants to play football, but her mother wants her to become a ballerina. Their clash of wills creates hilarious situations. Clever, delightful illustrations!
Printed Full Color
ISBN 0-933849-39-7

by Lisa Kirsten Butenhoff, age 13
Woodbury, Minnesota

The people of a Russian village face the winter without warm clothes or enough food. Then their lives are improved by a young girl's gifts. A tender story with lovely illustrations.
Printed Full Color
ISBN 0-933849-40-0

by Jennifer Brady, age 17
Columbia, Missouri

When poachers capture a pride of lions, a native boy tries to free the animals. A skillfully told story. Glowing illustrations illuminate this African adventure.
Printed Full Color
ISBN 0-933849-41-9

CONTEST FOR STUDENTS, Landmark Editions, Inc., P.O. Box 4469, Kansas City, MO 64127.

Jayna Miller
age 19

Lauren Peters
age 7

Michael Cain
age 11

Heidi Salter
age 19

Amity Gaige
age 16

Dennis Vollmer
age 6

Lisa Gross
age 12

Stacy Chbosky
age 14

Karen Kerber
age 12

David McAdoo
age 14

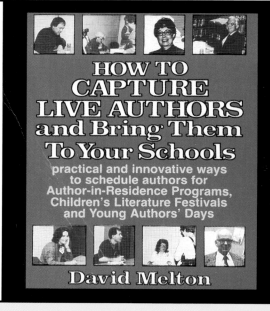